To my mother, in memory
of these events

The Christmas Train

by Ivan Gantschev

Translated from the German
by Karen M. Klockner

Little, Brown and Company
BOSTON   TORONTO

Many years ago, in a railroad station
high in the mountains, there lived
a stationmaster named Wassil
and his little daughter, Malina.

Wassil's job as stationmaster was to watch over the dangerous section of tracks that climbed high up into the mountains and passed through many dark tunnels.

One year on the afternoon of Christmas Eve,
Wassil went out to look over the tracks.
While he was gone, Malina trimmed the Christmas
tree with homemade decorations. She was excited
about the gift her father had promised her.

Suddenly she heard a terrible crash outside.
The dog started to bark and to scratch
at the door. "Oh, no!" cried Malina.
"That sounds like a rockslide!"

Malina rushed outside, and as she feared, a huge
rock had fallen on the tracks. She felt desperate.
"The Express comes in only half an hour!
What should I do?
What would Papa do?"
She tried to think clearly.
"I have to warn the engineer!"

Then she remembered something her father always
said: "If there is ever an obstruction on the tracks,
build a warning fire four hundred yards ahead of it
and wave a lantern."
Malina looked quickly around the room. Then,
without hesitating, she grabbed the Christmas tree –
decorations and all – and pulled the big lantern
down from its hook. With only a quarter of an hour
to spare, she rushed out the door.

Her heart pounding, Malina stumbled through the first tunnel carrying the glowing red lantern and dragging the Christmas tree. She kept running farther along the tracks until she could see the dark opening of the second tunnel. She could already hear the train coming.

There she stopped and set the Christmas tree on fire,
just as the Express was shooting out of the tunnel
and thundering furiously down the tracks. Up ahead of
him the engineer saw a brightly burning fire and a child
swinging a lantern. He was startled, but within an instant
he shut down the steam engine and pulled on the
emergency brake. The whistle blew, and the heavy train
came screeching and gasping to a halt.

Inside the train, in the dining car, everything tumbled into confusion: passengers, waiters, soup bowls, baked fish, and pastries. What a mess!

The huge, hissing train had stopped directly
in front of Malina. The engineer and the conductor
jumped down and ran toward the little
girl as she breathlessly exclaimed, "A huge rock has fallen
on the tracks up ahead! That's why I had to stop
the train." The two men were stunned.

Quickly the news of the rockslide spread through
the train, and soon everyone knew that a little girl
had saved them from a crash.
"The child is half frozen!" someone shouted, taking Malina
by the hand and leading her into the well-heated dining car.

Once inside, Malina saw the passengers whispering among themselves, and before she knew what was happening, they began to offer her some of their Christmas gifts. She was overwhelmed.

Then she looked up and saw her father standing in the door. In his arms he held a snowy white lamb. It was the Christmas gift he had promised her. As she ran up to him, he smiled proudly and said, "Come, Malina. It's time to go home."

Later that evening the conductor brought
them his own gift of thanks — a new Christmas
tree he had cut from along the tracks.
So Malina and her father could celebrate
Christmas at last.

ORIGINALLY PUBLISHED IN SWITZERLAND UNDER THE TITLE *DER WEIHNACHTSZUG*
COPYRIGHT © 1982 BY BOHEM PRESS, ZÜRICH, SWITZERLAND
ENGLISH LANGUAGE TEXT COPYRIGHT © 1984 BY LITTLE, BROWN AND COMPANY
ALL RIGHTS RESERVED. NO PART OF THIS BOOK MAY BE REPRODUCED
IN ANY FORM OR BY ANY ELECTRONIC OR MECHANICAL MEANS IN-
CLUDING INFORMATION STORAGE AND RETRIEVAL SYSTEMS WITHOUT
PERMISSION IN WRITING FROM THE PUBLISHER, EXCEPT BY A REVIEWER
WHO MAY QUOTE BRIEF PASSAGES IN A REVIEW.

LIBRARY OF CONGRESS CATALOG CARD NO. 84-80303

FIRST U.S. EDITION

PRINTED IN ITALY